Blastoff! Discovery launches a new mission: reading to learn. Filled with facts and features, each book offers you an exciting new world to explore!

This edition first published in 2020 by Bellwether Media, Inc.

No part of this publication may be reproduced in whole or in part without written permission of the publisher.
For information regarding permission, write to Bellwether Media, Inc., Attention: Permissions Department, 6012 Blue Circle Drive, Minnetonka, MN 55343.

Library of Congress Cataloging-in-Publication Data

Names: Polinsky, Paige V., author.
Title: The Bermuda Triangle / by Paige V. Polinsky.
Description: Minneapolis, MN : Bellwether Media, Inc., 2020.
  Series: Blastoff! Discovery : Investigating the Unexplained |
  Includes bibliographical references and index.
Identifiers: LCCN 2019001007 (print) | LCCN 2019015745
  (ebook) | ISBN 9781618915801 (ebook) |
  ISBN 9781644870396 (hardcover : alk. paper)
Subjects: LCSH: Bermuda Triangle–Juvenile literature.
Classification: LCC G558 (ebook) | LCC G558 .P65 2020
  (print) | DDC 001.94–dc23
LC record available at https://lccn.loc.gov/2019001007

Text copyright © 2020 by Bellwether Media, Inc. BLASTOFF! DISCOVERY and associated logos are trademarks and/or registered trademarks of Bellwether Media, Inc. SCHOLASTIC, CHILDREN'S PRESS, and associated logos are trademarks and/or registered trademarks of Scholastic Inc., 557 Broadway, New York, NY 10012.

Editor: Kate Moening   Designer: Andrea Schneider

Printed in the United States of America, North Mankato, MN.

TABLE OF CONTENTS

Risky Waters 4

Limbo of the Lost 8

Without a Trace 10

Searching the Depths 16

Sailing through Danger 24

The Triangle of Tomorrow 28

Glossary 30

To Learn More 31

Index 32

RISKY WATERS

Tiana watches the sky. Dark clouds are rolling in, but Charlie's eyes are glued to the computer. They are **investigating** the disappearance of the SS *Coyote*. One month ago, the cargo ship vanished just east of the Bahamas. Tiana and Charlie are searching for any sign of the *Coyote*. For now, it is one more **victim** of the Bermuda Triangle.

towed pinger locator

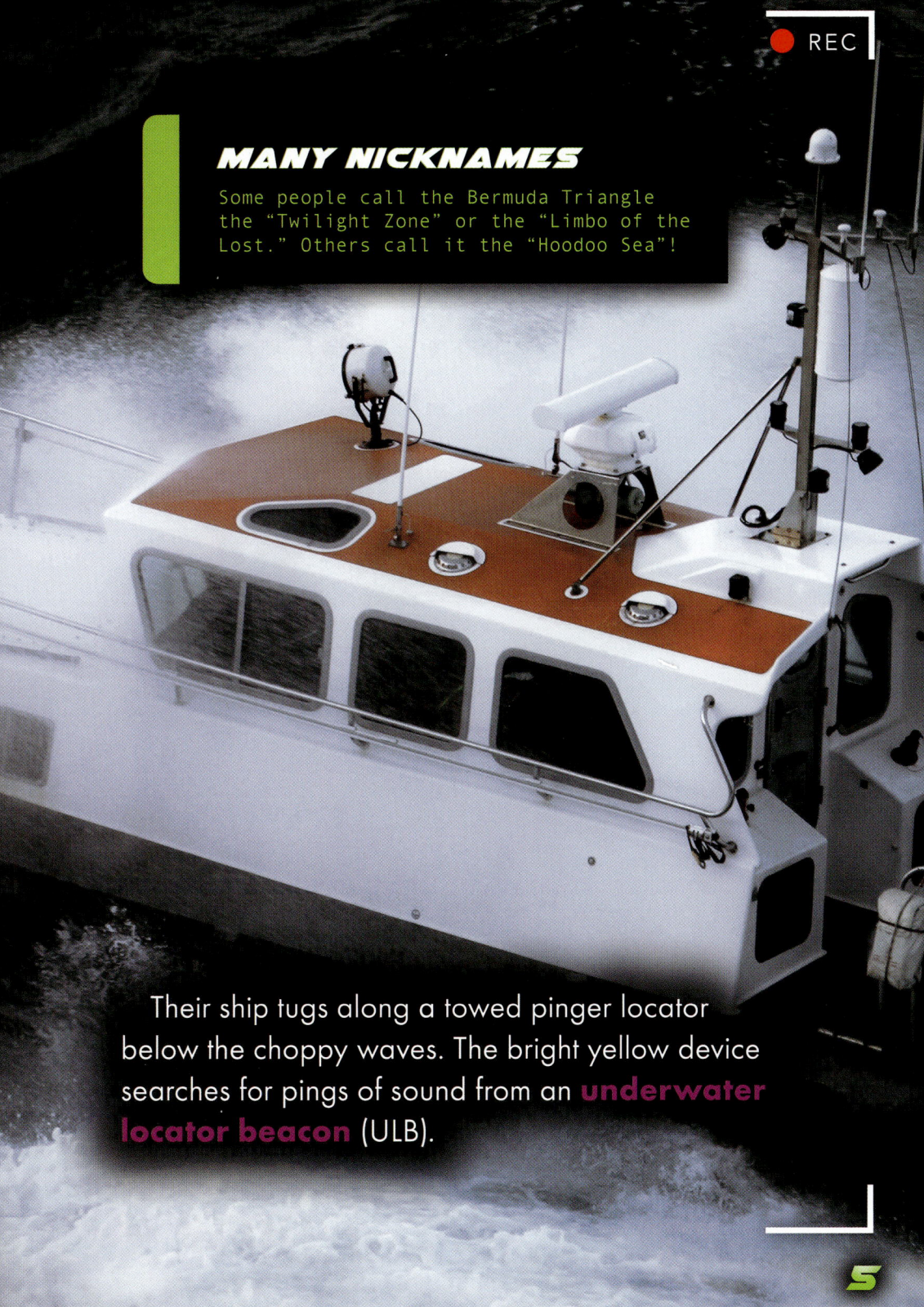

MANY NICKNAMES
Some people call the Bermuda Triangle the "Twilight Zone" or the "Limbo of the Lost." Others call it the "Hoodoo Sea"!

Their ship tugs along a towed pinger locator below the choppy waves. The bright yellow device searches for pings of sound from an **underwater locator beacon** (ULB).

A sudden noise makes the lines on the screen spike. Charlie leans over the computer screen, and Tiana slows the ship to a crawl. But the waves are getting choppier. Tiana can feel the wind speed picking up. "We need to get out of here," she says.

"No way!" Charlie taps the screen. "This is the strongest signal yet."

"So we come back tomorrow," Tiana says. Rough waves rock the ship back and forth. If the investigators are not careful, they might be the next to disappear in the Bermuda Triangle!

LIMBO OF THE LOST

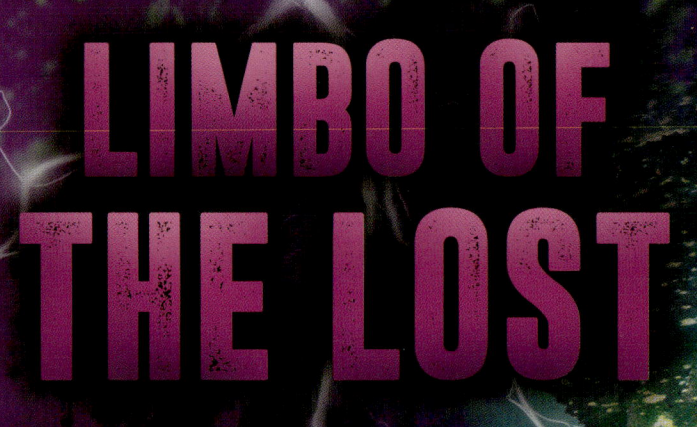

In the North Atlantic Ocean, one mysterious area is famous for its vanishing victims. It is known as the Bermuda Triangle. The Triangle's three points are commonly considered to be Florida, Bermuda, and Puerto Rico.

TRIANGLE TIME WARP

In 1970, pilot Bruce Gernon flew through a strange cloud in the Bahamas. He says it became a spinning tunnel! When Gernon escaped the fog, he had traveled much farther than he thought possible. He believes he survived a Triangle time warp!

BERMUDA TRIANGLE

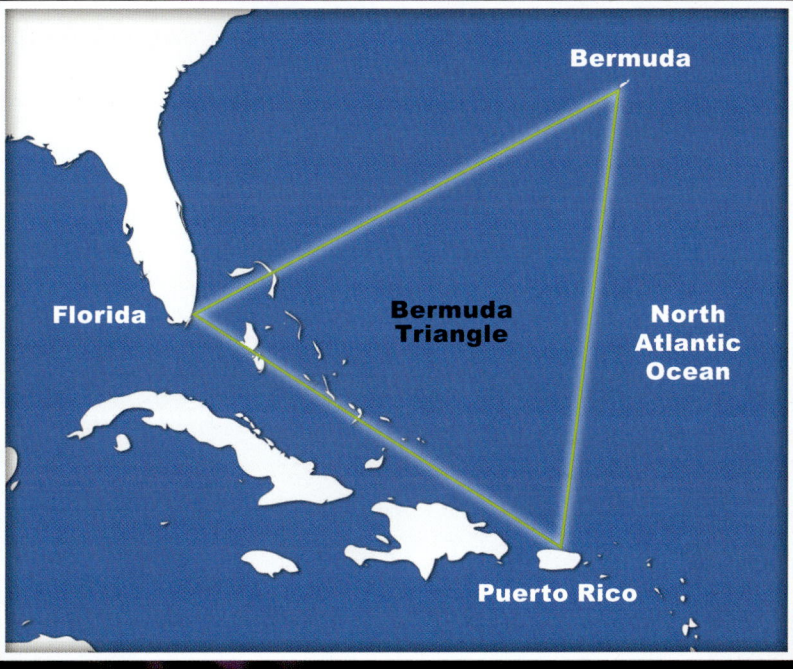

So far, more than 50 ships and 20 planes have vanished in the Triangle. Many people believe it is a **paranormal** mystery. Some say aliens, time warps, or sunken cities make the area extra dangerous!

WITHOUT A TRACE

The Bermuda Triangle holds centuries of mystery. But its first famous case happened in 1918. That February, the cargo ship USS *Cyclops* set out from Brazil to Maryland. Somewhere along the way, the giant ship disappeared along with more than 300 people on board.

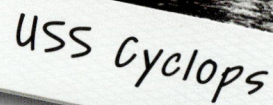

USS Cyclops

THE USS CYCLOPS

The USS *Cyclops* case remains the largest non-combat loss of life in Navy history. Some believed the ship was sunk by German spies. Others said it was captured by aliens or even eaten by a sea monster!

"Weather fair, all well."
 – Last radio message sent by the USS *Cyclops* crew

"Only God and the sea know what happened to the great ship."
 – President Woodrow Wilson

"There has been no more baffling mystery in...the Navy."
 – Official U.S. Navy Report

The *Cyclops* never sent a **distress call**, and the United States Navy radioed for days with no response. Investigators searched beaches and bays for **wreckage**. Divers hunted for clues below the waves. But no sign was ever found.

FACT MEETS FICTION

The Triangle also inspired many movies in the 1970s! Director Steven Spielberg included Flight 19 in his 1977 movie *Close Encounters of the Third Kind*.

pilots of Flight 19

In 1945, five Navy airplanes, known as Flight 19, went missing over the Bermuda Triangle. The seaplane sent to find them vanished too! Flight 19 became one of the most famous Triangle stories. It inspired many books about the Bermuda Triangle.

Authors shocked readers with tales from the Triangle. But pilot Larry Kusche blamed the mystery on bad research. He studied reports from the Navy and **U.S. Coast Guard**. He even flew over the Triangle himself! In 1975, Kusche released his first book. It showed that authors often changed important details about Triangle disappearances.

TBM Avenger, Flight 19 plane model

wave tank

Even with modern technology, ships continued to vanish in the Bermuda Triangle. But technology did help investigators find lost wreckage! In 2015, the cargo ship SS *El Faro* disappeared during a hurricane. Investigators found the sunken ship using **sonar** and underwater robots.

REGULAR VS ROGUE WAVES

The strength of a wave is measured in pounds per square inch (psi). Most modern ships can handle up to 21 psi without breaking.

- Large wave height: 39 feet (12 meters)
- Large wave breaking pressure: 8.5 psi
- Rogue wave height: up to 100 feet (30 meters)
- Rogue wave breaking pressure: 142 psi

El Faro was likely destroyed by a **rogue wave**. Scientist Simon Boxall studied these monster waves in 2018. His team tested a model of the USS *Cyclops* in a **wave tank**. They proved one rogue wave could snap a giant ship in two!

SEARCHING THE DEPTHS

In the past, Bermuda Triangle victims vanished without a trace. With no **evidence** to study, imaginations ran wild. But today's investigators have powerful tools to find lost ships.

Satellites can track a traveling ship or airplane's location. They can also measure weather activity in the area. This helps investigators decide where to search. Advanced search ships may also use wind and motion **sensors**. These keep investigators moving in the right direction through strong winds and waves.

DOWN, DOWN, DOWN...

The Bermuda Triangle is home to the deepest point in the Atlantic Ocean, the Milwaukee Depth. It is 27,493 feet (8,380 meters) below the ocean's surface!

Sonar finds evidence deep below the ocean's surface. A sonar device sends out pings of sound as it passes over the ocean floor. If the pings hit an object, they bounce back to the device. A computer uses these results to create images of the seafloor.

Searchers can investigate sonar results using remotely operated vehicles (ROVs). Investigators control these underwater robots from the surface. ROVs have cameras that send images to the ship through long cables. ROVs can quickly search deep, dark spaces for clues!

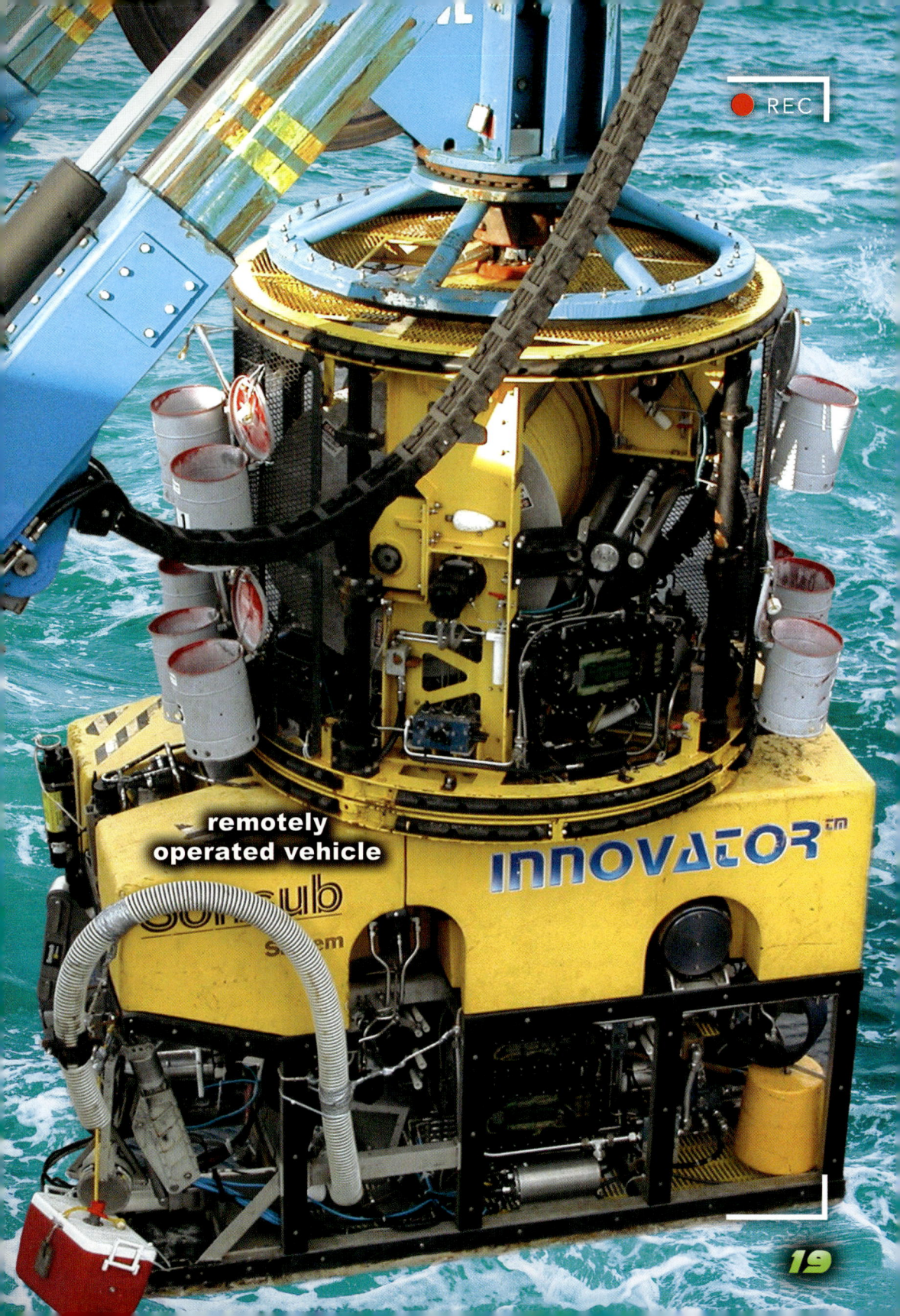

PINGER POWER

A towed pinger locator can find signals up to 20,000 feet (6,096 meters) away!

Many investigators hope to recover **data recorders**. Airplanes have one data recorder that tracks information like speed and height in the sky. Another records pilot voices and other cockpit sounds. Ship data recorders capture sounds and information like speed, location, and wind conditions.

recovered data recorder

Most data recorders have a ULB. When the ULB enters water, it sends out special sound waves. Investigators use towed pinger locators to hear these and find their source. Recovered data recorders may reveal key clues about a ship's final moments!

SS El Faro

PROFILE: FINDING THE SS EL FARO

The SS *El Faro* vanished on October 1, 2015, while sailing from Florida to Puerto Rico. Investigators listened for distress calls. They searched the sea for weeks. But the ship and its 33 crew members remained missing. Finally, on October 31, sonar found a ship 15,000 feet (4,572 meters) underwater. Searchers sent an ROV to look. It was *El Faro*!

In April, investigators recovered *El Faro*'s data recorder. They learned the ship was in poor shape before it set sail. *El Faro* was a terrible Bermuda Triangle accident. But it was not paranormal!

SAILING THROUGH DANGER

Each day, heavy traffic passes through the Bermuda Triangle peacefully. Some ships and planes do disappear. But **skeptics** say this is natural, not paranormal. Hurricanes are common in the Triangle, and powerful ocean currents cause sudden weather changes. These pose serious risks for travelers.

Several storms often hit the Triangle from different directions. This makes it a hotspot for rogue waves. They can destroy all evidence of a ship or airplane in minutes!

Skeptics argue that even in good weather, the Bermuda Triangle can be tricky to travel. It has many busy coastal areas. Rocks and reefs present hidden dangers. **Compasses** can be misread.

Many modern Triangle cases involve sailors and pilots with little training. They lack the tools and experience to travel safely. Skeptics point out that the number of Bermuda Triangle disappearances is similar in other busy ocean areas.

THE TRIANGLE OF TOMORROW

Will people continue disappearing in the Bermuda Triangle? It seems likely. The world's oceans are growing busier. Weather is becoming more dangerous. Heavier traffic and stronger storms might make the Triangle more of a risk for travelers.

But future cases may not stay closed for long. New technology makes it easier to track and contact ships in danger. Investigators will likely solve more and more cases. But will this wash away the tales of the Bermuda Triangle?

GLOSSARY

compasses—devices used to find direction by means of a needle that always points north

data recorders—electronic devices used in vehicles, ships, and airplanes to collect and log information related to a crash or accident

distress call—a signal, such as a radio code, used by a person, vehicle, or ship in need of emergency help

evidence—information that helps prove or disprove something

investigating—trying to find out the facts about something in order to learn if or how it happened

paranormal—unable to be explained by science

rogue wave—a large, sudden wave measuring more than twice the size of the waves around it

satellites—machines that orbit Earth, the moon, the sun, or a planet

sensors—devices that sense heat, light, sound, or motion and then react in a particular way

skeptics—people who doubt something is true

sonar—a device that uses sound waves to detect and map objects underwater

underwater locator beacon—a device that sends out sound waves to help searchers find a lost airplane or ship underwater

U.S. Coast Guard—an organization that guards the area along the country's coast and helps people, boats, and ships that are in danger on the sea

victim—someone who is harmed by an unpleasant event, such as an accident or illness

wave tank—a box filled with water and fitted with a machine that creates waves for study

wreckage—the broken or destroyed remains of an object

TO LEARN MORE

AT THE LIBRARY

Bowman, Chris. *Flight 19: Lost in the Bermuda Triangle*. Minneapolis, Minn.: Bellwether Media, 2020.

Jazynka, Kitson. *History's Mysteries: Curious Clues, Cold Cases, and Puzzles from the Past*. Washington, D.C.: National Geographic, 2017.

Levete, Sarah. *The Bermuda Triangle and Other Danger Zones*. New York, N.Y.: Gareth Stevens Publishing, 2017.

ON THE WEB

FACTSURFER

Factsurfer.com gives you a safe, fun way to find more information.

1. Go to www.factsurfer.com.

2. Enter "Bermuda Triangle" into the search box and click 🔍.

3. Select your book cover to see a list of related web sites.

INDEX

Bahamas, 4, 8
Bermuda, 8, 9
Boxall, Simon, 15
Brazil, 10
Close Encounters of the Third Kind, 12
compasses, 26
data recorders, 20, 21, 22
distress call, 11, 22
Flight 19, 12, 13
Florida, 8, 9, 22
Gernon, Bruce, 8
Kusche, Larry, 13
Maryland, 10
Milwaukee Depth, 18
nicknames, 5
North Atlantic Ocean, 8, 9, 18
Puerto Rico, 8, 9, 22
remotely operated vehicles, 18, 19, 22, 23
rogue wave, 15, 24
satellites, 16, 17
sensors, 16
skeptics, 13, 24, 26, 27
sonar, 14, 18, 22
SS *El Faro*, 14, 15, 22-23
tools, 4, 5, 6, 14, 16, 17, 18, 19, 20, 21, 22, 23, 26, 27, 28
towed pinger locator, 4, 5, 20, 21
traffic, 24, 28
underwater locator beacon, 5, 21
U.S. Coast Guard, 13
U.S. Navy, 11, 12, 13
USS *Cyclops*, 10, 11, 15
victim, 4, 8, 9, 10, 11, 12, 14, 16, 22
wave tank, 14, 15
weather, 6, 14, 16, 24, 25, 26, 28
wreckage, 11, 14, 23

The images in this book are reproduced through the courtesy of: Kletr, front cover (plane); PHOTO JUNCTION, front cover (ocean); Everett Collection, front cover (pilot); pingebat, front cover (map); Alexandra Tyukavina, pp. 2-3, 30-32; U.S. Navy/ Wiki Commons, pp. 4 (towed pinger locator), 22; ID-VIDEO, pp. 4-5; Denys Yelmanov, pp. 6-7; Anton Balazh, pp. 8-9; Bettmann/ Getty, p. 10 (USS Cyclops); Richard Whitcombe, pp. 10-11 (background); Time & Life Pictures/ Getty, pp. 12-13 (pilots); Stories in Light, p. 13 (TBM Bomber); Steve Exum, pp. 14-15; Phonlamai Photo, pp. 16-17 (satellite); aapsky, pp. 16-17 (Earth); Gulf of Mexico Deep Sea Habits Expedition/ Wiki Commons, pp. 18-19; Emilian Danaila, pp. 20-21 (pilot); Photography.co, pp. 20-21 (stormy sky); NTSB/ Alamy, p. 21 (data recorder); PJF Military Collection/ Alamy, p. 23 (all); NASA Photo/ Alamy, pp. 24-25; Maksimilian, pp. 26-27; Science Photo Library/ Alamy, pp. 28-29 (ocean); Who is Danny, pp. 28-29 (airplane).